dust
of eden

MARIKO NAGAI

ALBERT WHITMAN & COMPANY
CHICAGO, ILLINOIS

To DW and JNW

Nagai, Mariko.
Dust of Eden / by Mariko Nagai.
pages cm
Summary: "Thirteen-year-old Mina Tagawa and her Japanese American family
are forced to evacuate their Seattle home and are relocated to an internment
camp in Idaho, where they live for three years"—Provided by publisher.
1. Japanese Americans—Evacuation and relocation, 1942–1945—Juvenile
fiction. [1. Novels in verse. 2. Japanese Americans--Evacuation and relocation,
1942–1945—Fiction. 3. Family life—Fiction. 4. World War, 1939–1945—United
States—Fiction.] I. Title.
PZ7.5.N34Du 2014
[Fic]—dc23   2013033074

Text copyright © 2014 by Mariko Nagai
Published in 2014 by Albert Whitman & Company.
ISBN 978-0-8075-1739-0

Cover photo credit:
*Oakland, California. Kimiko Kitagaki, young evacuee guarding the family
baggage prior to departure . . ., 05/06/1942*, Dorothea Lange, 1942,
Courtesy of the National Archives, 537890, 210-G-C580

Cover design by Nick Tiemersma.

For more information about Albert Whitman & Company,
visit our web site at www.albertwhitman.com.

Imprisoned in here for a long, long time,
We know we're punished tho' we've committed no crime,
Our thoughts are gloomy and enthusiasm damp,
To be locked up in a concentration camp.

Loyalty we know and Patriotism we feel,
To sacrifice our utmost was our ideal
To fight for our country, and die mayhap;
Yet we're here because we happen to be a JAP.

We all love life, and our country best,
Our misfortune to be here in the West,
To keep us penned behind that DAMNED FENCE
Is someone's notion of NATIONAL DEFENCE!!!!!
DAMNED FENCE!
— *Unknown poet from Minidoka Concentration Camp*

Prologue

We held our breath for three
years. We did not have anything to call

our own except for the allowed number
of bags: two. We did not have anything

except for a rose garden my grandfather
made from hard earth and spit.

We lived behind a barbed wire
fence under a stark blue sky that could break

your heart (as it did break my grandfather's).
We lived under a sky so blue

in Idaho right near the towns of Hunt and Eden
but we were not welcomed there.

Through Sears & Roebuck catalogs
we lived outside of America.

Dust came through Eden, dust went
through our barracks, toward the sky,

westward, back to our home by the sea
in the city by the sea, in Seattle.

Part I. Seattle, Washington
OCTOBER 1941

The house is surrounded by roses
of all names: Bride's Dream, Chicago
Peace, Mister Lincoln, Timeless, Touch
of Class. The house is surrounded by hues
of red and white: red like an azure-sun,
red like the sunset over the Pacific Ocean,
red like Grandpa's fingertips,
white so transparent they call it Tineke,
the kind of white that looks like Seattle on a rainy day.

The living room is a mixture of East
and West: Grandpa packed a little of Japan
when he came here across the sea—a sword,
a photograph of himself as a small boy,
dolls for future daughters he never had—
memories of his once-ago life.

Grandpa is a rose breeder.
He calls roses *bara*; he calls them his *kodomo*—children.
My father sometimes helps out Grandpa,
though most of the time, he works in an office
downtown writing articles for a newspaper.

Mother sits in the kitchen, always singing.
My room upstairs is All American: a bed,
an old desk, white lace curtains my mother sewed,
pictures of Jamie and me on the wall.

My brother Nick's room next to mine is filled
with trophies he won in track races.
Grandpa calls me by my middle name, *Masako*,
and he calls Nick *Toshio*. He never speaks
English; says that he lived longer in Japan
than he has in America, and that there's no more
space for another language or culture.

He speaks to us in Japanese, my parents speak
to him in Japanese, and Nick and I speak
some words in Japanese, but mostly in English.
Just like our breakfast, rice and pickled
plums with milk and potatoes, they all mix together.

DECEMBER 1941

I was singing with the Sunday school
choir, practicing our Christmas carols,

all our mouths opening and closing as one
to sing the next note.

We were singing "Silent Night, Holy
Night," and just as the boys hit

their lowest key, the door burst
open like a startled cat dashing.

The next note lay waiting
under Mrs. Gilbert's finger; our mouths kept

the O shape, when a man yelled, *the Japs bombed
Pearl Harbor*. The world stopped.

The next words got lost. *Oh, oh, oh,*
someone wailed, until I realized that it was

coming out of my mouth,
my body shaking, trembling.

And the world started again
but we were no longer singing as one.

DECEMBER 1941

Jap, Jap, Jap, the word bounces
around the walls of the hall.

Jamie, my best friend, yells out, "Shut your
mouth!" but the word keeps

bouncing like a ball in my head.
As soon as I get to my Language

Arts class, the entire class gets quiet.
Mrs. Smith looks down

like she's been talking about me,
or maybe she doesn't see me.

She clears her voice; she calls
out our names, one by one; she pauses

right after Marcus Springfield.
She clears her throat, calls out *Mina Tagawa*.

And instead of calling out Joshua
Thomas, she starts to talk

about what happened yesterday.
My face becomes hot and heavy; I look

at my hands, then at the swirling
pattern on the desk. I look at my hands again,

yellowish against the dark brown
desk, and Jamie's hair, golden,

right near it. *Jap-nese*, Mrs. Smith
starts. *Jap-nese* have attacked Pearl

Harbor. *Jap-nese* have broken
the treaty. *Jap-nese* have started the war.

Even the newspaper that Father works for screams in
bold letter headlines: *Japs. Japs. Japs.*

I feel everyone's eyes on me. I hear
Chris Adams snickering behind me, whispering

*Jap Mina. I'm not
Japanese*, I want to yell.

I am an American, I scream
in my head, but my mouth is stuffed

with rocks; my body is a stone, like the statue
of a little Buddha Grandpa prays to

every morning and every night. My body is heavy.
I don't know how to speak anymore.

DECEMBER 1941

We are not Americans, the eyes tell us.
We do not belong, the mouths curl up.

We are the enemy aliens, the Japs,
the ones who have bombed

Pearl Harbor, killing so many soldiers
who were enjoying their Sunday

morning in Hawaii, who were waking
up to their breakfasts of oatmeal and toast.

Death to Japs, they say. The voice
from the radio says *Jap-nese*,

a pause between *Jap*
and *nese*, just like Mrs. Smith.

Mother walks down Main Street with her head
up, her back straight, though

men spit at her and women hiss
at her. *Masa-chan, Onnanoko rashiku*

sesuji o nobashina-sai. (Masako,
keep your back straight like a

good girl), Mother says as she pulls
on the whitest kid gloves,

one by one, stretching her fingers
straight to sheath each finger.

Masa-chan, tebukuro
hamenasai. Amerika-jin wa

sahou ni kibishii kara. (Masako,
put on your gloves. Americans

are strict with manners), Mother says
as she straightens her jacket.

We pass by the stores that sell
oatmeal and toast and go to Mr. Fukuyama's shop:

Patriotic Americans, says a sign on the window.
She buys a bag of rice and *umeboshi* and bonito

flakes. If I could, I would keep
only my first name, *Mina,* my American name,

and tear off *Masako Tagawa* like the
pages of journals I tore out when I found

out that Nick Freeman liked Alice
Gorka. I would change my hair color into a honey

blond that changes into lighter
shades of almost white during the summer,

just like Jamie's. If I could change
my name, if I could change my parents,

I could change my life: I would be an American.
But I already am.

DECEMBER 1941

We're best friends, no matter what, Jamie
   says as we sit under the Christmas

tree together. *We're best friends until
   we die,* I say.

She hands me a small packet wrapped
   in a bright red wrapping paper.

Open it, open it, she urges. Mr. Gilmore's humming
   drifts in from his workshop in

the backyard, and Mrs. Gilmore's baking
   smells of cinnamon and nutmeg.

We sit under a big Christmas tree lit by small twinkling
   lights like lost fireflies late in summer.

A package the size of my palm, so light like a butterfly;
   Jamie chanting, *Open it, open it!*

I undo the ribbon gingerly, then unfold the red
   paper, one corner at a time. In the middle,

a jagged half of a heart. She pulls her sweater
   down, *See, I have half a heart, too.*

And whenever we are together, we have a whole heart.
   Only then do the two halves become one.

DECEMBER 1941

When I come home, the house is quiet.
    Basho is outside, looking confused.

Mother is not home, where she always is,
    waiting with a cup of green tea between

her hands and a glass of milk for me.
    Everything is turned inside

out, rice scattered all over the kitchen
    floor, all the drawers wide open

with cloth strewn all over the floor
    like garbage the day after the circus

left town. A note, *I will be back soon*,
    in Mother's beautiful and careful handwriting

pinned to the door like a dead butterfly.
    It is only later, too late for dinner,

too late for a glass of milk and cup of tea,
    when Mother and Grandpa come home

looking like they are carrying the night
    on their backs, their bodies heavy

from the weight they drag through
    the door. *Men came this afternoon,*

they said they are from the government;
     your father had to go with them so he can

answer some questions, Mother says quietly
     as she sits down on the sofa, heavily

throwing her weight down. *When is he coming home?*
     I ask. Basho mewls, climbs next

to Grandpa, pressing his body so close that his tail
     curled around the bend in Grandpa's

skinny body. *I'm not sure, honey, I'm just
     not sure,* Mother says quietly.

Grandpa takes his owl-like glasses off slowly,
     presses his eyes with the palms

of his hand like he was pressing down the dirt
     around his rose trees, and leans back

on his rocking chair. Mother leans back, too.
     I sit, the word *war* ringing

through my head, forgetting about milk,
     forgetting about dinner, forgetting about

history homework, thinking only about Father
     in prison.

JANUARY 1942

This year, there wasn't a
Christmas tree, or dinner with
our neighbors.
There weren't any New Year's
festivities this year,
no mochi—sticky rice—
no giving of money or playing games.
Without Father's face red as a beet
from sake, and Grandpa
singing as he plays
the *shamisen*—the three
stringed lyre made out
of a skin of virgin cat—
there is no laughter, no joy.
Mother hurries from the dining
room to the kitchen,
sleeves of her kimono
fluttering
like a humming bird's
wings. All is quiet in this
house, with its small
ornament of bamboo
and pine branches
Grandpa left hanging
on my door.
Happy New Year it is not.

JANUARY 1942

Father looks small
sitting behind the bars,
surrounded by
soldiers towering
over him. He smiles,
then coughs, once,
twice. He asks me
how I am, whether
I've been a good girl,
and have obeyed my elders.
He squints his eyes,
his eyes bigger without
his glasses.
Mother gives him *nigiri*
—rice balls—and he smiles,
saying that the food
they serve him is too oily,
too *American*. I ask him
how he is, a stupid question,
I know, but he looks so small,
and so tired,
that's the only thing
I can think to ask him. *Fine,* he whispers,
Everything is going to be fine,
they'll figure out, soon, that this
is unconstitutional.
We are led away
only thirty minutes later,
our footsteps echoing in the hallway,

the door banging,
then locking behind us,
my father left alone
in prison like a caged bird.

JANUARY 1942

Every time I walk down the hall
at school, kids hiss *Jap*
Jap. Every time I walk home
from school, I feel eyes as heavy
as handcuffs around my wrists and ankles.
Every time Mother and I go downtown
in our Ford to shop at Mr. Fukuyama's
grocery store, every time Mother says
Konnichiwa, I look away.
Every time I see the word *Jap* in newspapers,
I become hot. Every time Mother cooks
miso soup and rice for dinner, suddenly
I am not hungry. Every time I see
myself in the mirror, I see a slant-eyed
Jap, just like they say, my teeth protruding
like a rat's. Every time I look away,
Jamie holds my hand.

FEBRUARY 1942

Dear Father, I hope
everything is okay
and that you are
doing well.
From the letters
you sent us,
the parts we can read
that haven't been
blacked out, it seems
that they are treating
you well. Here, at home,
Grandpa's been
pulling us together,
saying now that you are
in Montana (or North
Dakota, or wherever
they took you), we have
to listen to him.
Don't tell Nick I told
you this, but a week ago,
Grandpa found out Nick's been
breaking the curfew,
and without saying a word,
as soon as Nick came home,
Grandpa raised his cane
and hit him hard, once,
twice, over the head.
Nick just stood there,
angry, with his fists raised,

but he didn't say or do anything
as Grandpa kept hitting him
again and again with his cane.
Mom was crying, and shouting,
Oto-san, yamete, yamete
– Father, stop it, stop it –, and
I was frozen, right there.
I've never seen this
Grandpa, who was like a stranger, angry
and spiteful. But as soon
as Nick apologized (for what?),
Grandpa stopped.
Okami o okoraseruna – Don't anger the government –,
Grandpa said slowly.
But we didn't do anything wrong, Nick shouted.
We're American, just like everyone else.
Grandpa shook his head,
ware ware wa Nipponjin demo naishi,
Americajin demo nai—we are neither
Japanese nor American. His words stung me,
stronger than bee stings, even stronger
than the news of Pearl Harbor.
I went up the dark stairs
holding Basho in my arms
and shut my door and shut my eyes.
Most of the time, we are
doing okay, but Seattle's changed.
Chinese kids walk around with buttons
that say, "I am Chinese."

Then there are all these signs:
We don't serve Japs. Japs go home.
The entire country hates
Japan. And they hate us.
No one seems to like us
anymore, except for Jamie
and her parents, Mr. and Mrs. Gilmore.
Nick doesn't say
it, but he's having a really
hard time, I can tell.
He comes home with bruises
and cuts, and when Mother asks
him what happened, he only says
that he fell. I know he's lying,
I know he knows that I know,
but we don't talk about it.
How other boys push him around,
doesn't matter he was voted the Most Popular,
they call him Tojo, Jap, Rat, and he answers
each and every curse with a punch.
Mother tells me not to go out
by myself. It's hard to walk
down the street, being different.
I hope the new glasses Mother sent
you are the kind you like.
I miss you very much. I hope they are
treating you well. Father, I hope
you can come home soon so we can
all be together. I miss you.
Your daughter, Masako

FEBRUARY 1942

President Roosevelt
signed Executive
Order 9066 today. Nick says
that Germans and Italians
aren't arrested like
Japanese men have been all over
the West Coast. *Mina,*
he whispered in the back
yard, *they'll put us
all in prisons.*
I don't want to believe him,
but I see Grandpa
and Mother worrying over our
frozen bank accounts and
curfews and blackouts
and the five-mile radius, and I know
we will probably be put in
prison just like they did Father.

MARCH 1942

Grandpa sits on his favorite chair right near the rose
garden. His face, from where I stand, is as big as

the roses all around him, roses of bright red, deep red,
blood red, all kinds of red only he knows the names

for. *Masako, chotto kinasai*, he calls me over as he hears
the gate opening. He does not turn around. He does

not look at me, but keeps looking ahead, at his roses,
at the sky, at everything but me. Basho stretches

on Grandpa's lap, then jumps down, saunters over to me,
and says hello by twirling his tail around my legs.

Grandpa, without moving his mouth, says, *We have
been asked to leave. We need to pack up*

*everything: the house, the nursery. We can only take two
pieces of luggage per person. We need to leave soon. And*

I'm sorry, we can't take Basho. I am not hearing him
right, I tell myself. Why do we need to move?

*They say that they are doing this for our safety. They say
that we will be taken care of. They say that it's for our own
good.*

Ware ware no tame da, Grandpa says quietly in Japanese.
He reaches over, then taking a pair of scissors,

snips off a bud.
Ware ware no tame da, he repeats again. I know

that's a lie. I know they are doing this to hurt us. But I do
not say anything at all. *Ware ware no tame da,*

his words echo in my head.
It's for our own good, he says. Or so they say.

APRIL 1942

We have one week
to get ready.
It's only been one week
since Mother and Grandpa
went to the Japanese
American Citizens League
Office and registered us
to be evacuated
to a place called Camp
Puyallup somewhere
not far away.
We are to leave
on Thursday, April
30th. Not a single Japanese
is to stay in Seattle
after May 1.
Mother and Grandpa
told us we are not
selling the house
like other families,
but that we'll board it up,
and that we'll be back.
We have a week to say

good-bye, a week
to pack everything up.
It's a week that
seems not long
enough,
but forever.

APRIL 1942

What I can take:
    the Bible that Mother gave me for my 12th birthday
    my journals
    Jamie's Christmas present
    homework assignments for the rest of the semester
    (in case I return to Garfield next September)
    clothes for autumn (maybe for winter, too)
    the things that the WRA has ordered us to take:
    blankets and linen; a toothbrush, soap,
    also knives, forks, spoons, plates, bowls and cups.

What I cannot take:
    Basho
    our house
    Jamie
    the choir
    Grandpa's rose garden
    Seattle and its sea-smell

What my Grandfather packs:
    a potted rose

APRIL 1942

Basho is old.
The mangy
orange kitten
with a broken tail
came to the front
steps on a rainy
day and no matter
how much Grandpa shooed
it away, the cat kept
mewing until
Grandpa got sick
of it and pulled him
from under the porch
by the scuff
of his neck
and stuffed him
into the bed
next to him.
Fleas got
Grandpa, but Basho got
Grandpa. Basho came
when I was five.
See that scar
on his cheek?
He got it fighting
Kuro from four
houses down; he won.
See how his left
ear is torn? He got

it fighting
crows that were in the roses.
Basho brings gifts;
don't be surprised.
Birds. Squirrels. Baby
moles. Basho likes
to have his ears
pulled gently.
He'll show you
his belly if you do
that. He doesn't understand
English; he grew
up around us, listening to
Japanese. He doesn't drink
milk. He grew up drinking
miso soup and eating bonito
flakes and rice.
He is a good cat.
Please take care
of him. He'll love
you, like he loves us,
like we love
him, like I love you. Jamie.

APRIL 1942

Mother stands
in the middle
of the room,
our sofas
and table
and chairs
covered in
white sheets
looking like Halloween
ghosts.
She walks,
the sound of
her bare footsteps
across
the bare floor
empty, up
the bare steps
to my room,
where she puts me to sleep
on a blanket
on the floor.
It is cold;
I never knew
our house could
be so cold.

APRIL 1942

The nursery is dismantled,
each glass pane taken off
from the frame. All the windows
of our house are boarded up;
the car's inside the garage.
Everything has been put into
boxes and crates and stored
in the garage or with the Gilmores.
My room is bare except
for the naked bed and an empty
dresser draped in white; it's
my very own ghost.
Mr. Gilmore shakes his head
as Mother gives him the keys,
"I don't know what the world
is coming to, but don't worry,
we'll take care of everything.
They'll realize how silly all this
is, and you'll be back here
before you know it." Mother bows
deeply, her shoulders trembling
like a feather, and Mrs. Gilmore
puts her arm around Mother, she, too,
shaking. Mr. Gilmore opens
the door to his truck
where the back is filled
with our bags. Grandpa stands
in front of our house, feeling
the bark of the cherry blossom

tree he planted when I was
born, feeling it, stroking it,
gently, as he looks at the house,
at the space where the nursery
used to be, then he raises his hat,
tips it gently, saying goodbye
to everything, to the house, to the wintering
roses left behind that will probably die
without his care, and to the tree
that has begun to bud.

APRIL 1942

Chinatown,
where all the
Japanese stores
used to be, is
boarded up.
It's a ghost town;
no one's about so early
in the morning.
It's a ghost town
now and maybe forever.
A sign:
Thank you for your patronage,
it was a pleasure to serve you
for the past twenty years.
Then it gets smaller and smaller
and finally disappears
as we drive
quickly
toward the junction
of Beacon Avenue
and Alaska Street
at the southern end
of Jackson Park.

APRIL 1942

We are all tagged like parcels,
    our bags, our suitcases,
    my mother, me, Nick, Grandpa.
    Tagged with numbers, we have become
    numbers, faceless, meaningless.

We were told to come to Jackson Park,
    just two suitcases each,
    no more names, no memories, no Basho,
    only ourselves and what we can carry.

Here we are, waiting for the buses
    to arrive, photographers flashing and clicking,
    other Japanese like us, so many,
    all quietly waiting, wordlessly smiling,
    without resistance.

And we all shiver because it is cold,
    because we do not know where we are
    going, because we are leaving
    home as the enemy.

Part II. "Camp Harmony,"
Puyallup Assembly Center, Puyallup, Washington
APRIL 1942

I fell asleep against a hard and unyielding
Nick, rigid with his anger, as the bus trembled,
shook like an old woman, like the rocking of a crib,
and we all slept like children, lost, not

sure where we were going. We were all
brothers and sisters, cousins and more,
our hair black, our skin yellow. No
one ever told me that there are so many

shades of yellow, that some of us aren't
even yellow and slant-eyed
like the newspapers show.
We got on the bus this morning.

We packed our bags last night.
Jamie came with her Mom, like she promised,
and I smiled, though I wanted to cry,
my smile hard on my face like

a cracking plate. Soldiers yelled at us
angrily, *Get on the bus, quickly,*
pushing an old man into a bus with the butt
of their rifles; *Japs go home*, a redneck yelled, his voice
piercing the crowd.

Outside the bus, the sea of heads,
black, blond, brown, red, straight, wavy,
curly, all waving, yelling, smiling, hiding tears.
I leaned out the window and yelled, *Jamie, take*

care of Basho, Basho likes to be
rubbed on his belly, but be careful of his claws.
Jamie nodded and held out the broken heart,
I promise I will, I promise!

Grandpa sat quietly next to Mother, looking ahead,
his potted rose on his lap. Nick sat next to me,
his eyes as hard as his fists. *Americans don't*
keep promises, you remember that, Mina, he hisses.

I waved goodbye, and Jamie waved and didn't stop,
yelling promises that she'd write.
I remember Jamie's dad with his jolly made-up face,
Jamie's mom pressing a handkerchief to her eyes,
Jamie next to them, waving her arm
in a circle, mouthing something.

Then the first bus started to move, and
everyone became quiet. People outside.
People inside. All of us quiet,
so very quiet that it seemed we were watching an ancient
movie from the 1920s, where people cried without sound.

We were all sad, but put on smiling faces, like we did not care, like our hearts were not breaking, though if you listened hard, if you ignored the engines, you could hear thousands of hearts breaking, shattering, into pieces.

APRIL 1942

They open
our bags,
one by one,
those soldiers
with rifles
and hard eyes,
taking out this
and that,
holding up
Mother's underwear
and mine, too.
Mother looks
away, her face
bright red;
mine is so hot
I think I'll burst.
They probe
me from head
to toe,
searching my
head for lice,
listening
to my lungs
for whistling,
for *tuberculosis*
they say,
examining
my hands
for dirt

or warts.
They pry open
Grandpa's mouth
and ask him
to remove
his dentures,
which Grandpa
does without
a word,
his face collapsing
like a withering rose
as soon as
his teeth lie
on the palm
of the soldier's hand.
Nick is next
but he just
stands there
stubbornly,
not taking off
his shirt,
not taking
off his hat,
just standing
there stoically
like a rock,
like a stubborn
stone that cannot
be moved,
no matter how hard
they try.

APRIL 1942

They have taken away Mother's well-thumbed bible.
  They have taken away her diaries written in Japanese.

They have taken away Grandpa's scrapbooks of flowers.
  They have taken away his Japanese-English dictionary.

They have taken away our books, *Manyoshu, Tales of Genji,*
  They have taken away Nick's laughter and jokes.

They have taken away Father and black-lined his letters.
  They have taken away our homes, our words, my father.

MAY 1942

A stall that smells of a horse
that isn't here. Hay everywhere,
scattered by long gone hooves.
They call it Camp Harmony, a former
fair site flattened down by horses' hooves.
They give us big sacks and tell us to gather
as much hay as we can
so we can stuff them and sleep on them.
It's only temporary, that's what they say.
We'll be home before Christmas.
Kids laugh and eat ice cream outside
the store across the barbed wire fence.
Guards look down on us with rifles
pointing at us, yelling for us to "stay away
or we'll shoot." Horses are gone.
We're the new cattle.

MAY 1942

Dear Jamie,

    Thank you, thank you, thank you
for coming to see me last Sunday!
When I got your letter saying that
you and your parents would come to visit,
I was so happy I couldn't sleep
the entire week. And the night before
you came, I cleaned as much as I could
(though our new home is so small,
and Mother being the way she is,
there wasn't much to clean),
made sure we had enough coffee
and tea (we don't have orange juice
here at the camp). Oh, when I saw
you and your family standing outside
the fence, my heart jumped!
Even Nick seemed to remember his Seattle
self (he's been angry, you know, with
the move and all). We thought you'd all
be allowed in, so it was awkward when
we had to stand inside the fence
and you all out; Mom was really embarrassed.
Tell your dad how happy Grandpa was
to hear that some of his roses are thriving
under his care; please tell your mom
how much we're still enjoying all the cakes
and cookies she baked for us. (Too bad
that the guards broke most of the cookies
when they ripped open the box. Did they think

you were bringing us guns or something?) Anyway,
I hope your dad's not upset anymore; I've never
seen him so angry. It's not as bad as he thinks,
once you get used to it. Even the smell, I'm beginning to like.
I miss you already, I do.

      Your best friend, Mina

MAY 1942

Today, rumor has it,
a Japanese man was shot
to death as he tried
to escape from a camp
in Oklahoma, or was it Montana?
His name was Ichiro Shimoda.
Ichiro, the first son.
Somewhere
his parents must be crying.
Somewhere, his second and third
brothers—Jiro and Saburo—must
be crying. Today it rained in Camp
Puyallup. Today, in Oklahoma,
or somewhere far away, it
rained one man, who fell
to the ground and turned
the ground red.

MAY 1942

A dandelion
pokes out
from the floor
board, pushing
into our room
as someone
next door
snores.

JUNE 1942

Today, it's raining
outside as well
as inside,
and no matter
how many times we
place the cups
and bowls
and plates under
the drips,
they become full
as soon as
we empty them
out. The floor
is muddy, so muddy
that we wear
shoes inside.

JUNE 1942

Why are we here, what did we do
that they had to send us to a place
fit for horses? There is no hot water,
and there's no real toilet except for a hole
in the ground. Everyone smells bad, the toilets smell
worse, every room smells like horses and horse dung.
We have become like cows—the guards even talk to us
as if we're cows: slowly, with each word exaggerated.
There are bugs everywhere, inside the mattresses, around
the toilets, and my body itches so much I can't keep from
scratching and scratching, my body covered with scabs.
And food. Free. But I don't want to smell any more
canned corn, wieners and pork. I want rice.
I want miso soup. I want Basho.
I want to sleep in my own bed.
I want to be called Jap,
I would endure it if that would take me home.

JULY 1942

Standing in the line
in the rain to eat
at the canteen, only to find
overcooked vegetables
and canned sausages.
Food all slopped onto
one plate, sauces mixing
and mashed, only to find
no seat next to Mom
or Nick, and I have to eat
with a strange family,
all by myself, like an orphan.
Grandpa pushing
away the dishes, sighing,
getting skinnier and skinnier
each day because he cannot eat the food.
Nick does not come
home all day, and when he does,
he brings with him dark clouds
so thick that the room itself
becomes one dark room
where no on speaks, and no one smiles.
Why should we celebrate
Independence Day when we don't have it?

Part III. Minidoka Relocation Center,
Hunt, Idaho
AUGUST 1942

When they said we were to move,
we traveled for a day and half on the cattle train,

in darkness, scared, because someone said
that once we get to Idaho, they'd line us up

and shoot us, one by one. We got off in the middle
of the never-ending dry field with our luggage

piled up high with tags flapping in the wind.
Our bodies creaked and we were bone tired; we looked

around and saw nothing, lots and lots of nothing.
When we got on the bus, we were not expecting

the land to be so flat the horizon went on and on
from east to west. We were not expecting a land so dry,

so parched, that our steps kicked up dust,
swallowing our feet like a hungry animal.

We passed people who welcomed us,
huddling by the gate like winter pigeons in the sun.

Grandpa held my hand tight but he did not
talk. Mother's mouth opened once, then closed,

her words lost somewhere between sadness and shock.
She did not open it until we signed ourselves

into Minidoka Relocation Camp, not until we saw
our room so small, with four army cots and a pot-belly stove.

Grandpa held on to his pot of roses and sat
down on a suitcase as weathered and cracked

as his own face. Nick looked down at his shoes, following
the pattern of uneven boards with his toes.

Mother finally opened her mouth, and said, "This is
our new home," in a voice hard, hard as granite, hard as the ground.

I stood there, next to Mother, and saw her face trembling,
contorting, and echoed her words, this time as a question.

"This is our new home?" We were not expecting heaven.
We were not expecting anything like our real home in Seattle,

but we were hoping for something more than this.
Grandpa whispered,

Korekara koko ga ie da
This is our home from now on.

SEPTEMBER 1942

Here in Minidoka, everything changes in front of our eyes:
    the earth that is dry and yellow
turns into barb-wired sky and the guards staring
    down at us with rifles in their hands.

A life that was simple, going to school, coming
    back home, a warm home and a flushing
toilet turned into a darker, night-like place,
    where there are more shadows than light.

The dry land that greeted us when we first arrived
    has turned into moist land,
and instead of tumbleweeds roaming the streets
    men and women stroll hand in hand, laughing.

And the room, when we first entered, with wind blowing
    hard between the cracks, turned into
something bearable, a home, but not quite,
    but home nevertheless.

And the city by the sea, our home on Sycamore Street,
    my friends at Garfield, my teachers' names,
the walk on the paved streets, the downtown,
    all that, seems like a wonderful dream. But only a dream.

SEPTEMBER 1942

Dear Jamie,
  Thank you for the books you sent me,
  and please thank your mom for the cookies
  and your dad for the seeds.
  School hasn't started yet; there aren't any teachers
  or even any rooms to teach in. I guess if you live in
  the middle of nowhere, you can't get teachers to
  apply, and even worse, you can't get anyone to teach
  us. Remember how we wished that we didn't have to go
  to school? Well, I got my wish but now, I wish that I
  could go to class instead. Everything is so basic,
  you'd think we lived somewhere in Africa, not
  America. It's so dusty here we all walk around
  covering our mouths and noses. The toilets are still
  just holes in the ground; they tell us to make
  as much sound as we can before using them, since it's
  not unusual to see a black widow spider or a rattlesnake.
  All we do is stand in line: to use the
  bathroom, to take a shower (if we can), to get our
  meals. The other day, Grandpa and I stood by the
  fence, and the guards all started screaming, *Get away
  from the fence, stay the damn away from the fence
  or we'll shoot.* Something just snapped, and I don't
  know what happened, but I screamed back, *What are you
  going to do, shoot us?* Grandpa kept bowing and bowing,
  Masako, ayamare, hayaku ayamare. Matsuko, apologize,
  apologize quickly, but I went a little bit crazy.
  The guards looked at each other, their rifles still
  pointing at us, Grandpa kept bowing and bowing,

but I glared at them. *We didn't do anything wrong,*
I yelled. Grandpa gave me a scolding when we got
back, but I don't regret what I did. Nick said
that he was proud of me, but to be careful, because of
that kid that was shot. Maybe I shouldn't have. I don't
know anymore.

Yours, Mina (Masako)

SEPTEMBER 1942

Line after line.   To the mess hall.   To
the bathroom. To sign our lives in.
          To sign ourselves out.   To eat.   To
bathe.   To talk, to send letters.

Line after line,   snaking around
          the barracks,   around the streets,   and
over the streets,

          barbed wires

Separating us from rest of the world,

Lines that push us in.   Push us away.
          Lines to get   into the bus.
Lines to evacuate us.   Lines that border us in,
to say who belongs
          where, who we are,

A line that stretches from north to south,   a horizon.

OCTOBER 1942

There is no room I can call my own.
My mother, Nick, Grandpa and I are all in the same room.
The Akagis are next door, separated from us by a thin
wall of a board, and everything they do we can hear.

No one talks; no one laughs. We stand in line.

When Nick leaves our room, he leaves behind a dark
thunder cloud. He has carried the gloom
with him for so long that it has become a part
of him and has settled in shadows of the room.

No one talks; no one laughs. We stand in line.

Complete darkness after ten p.m. There is nowhere
to hide here; the eyes of the guard towers, with their bright
beams, roam nightly. Everyone's sighs, worries, and com-
plaints fly through the night air, entering through the gaps.

No one talks; no one laughs. We stand in line.

Someone's dream enters into me. We dream the same dreams,
dreams of home and of going home, but when
the morning comes, the dreams are simply dreams, and give
way to sadness and days becoming one, standing in lines.

No one talks; no one laughs. We stand in line.

OCTOBER 1942

Dust enters
during the night like a thief,
leaving mounds
of sand in all corners
of the room where the wind left it,
leaving mounds like graves,
even on top of us, burying us
while we were asleep.
Dust enters through our noses
and mouths while we are asleep,
when we talk, when we breathe,
in this place just a few miles away from Eden,
where they know nothing of our lives,
where they know nothing of the people
who live behind the machine
guns and barbed wires,
buried in sand each and every morning.

NOVEMBER 1942

Dear Father,

A baby's been born.
  The newspaper story said, "Emily

Harumi Shimada was born last night at 8:49 pm.
  The mother and baby are in good

health. The father, Charles 'Chuck' Shimada,
  is in D.C. working for the Foreign Services."

All the women
  walking around with laundry baskets

carried them as if they were
  carrying around babies of their own.

When I told Grandpa about the baby,
  Grandpa smiled

and told me that Harumi meant *Spring Sea*.
  But the first thing she's going to see

is the barbed wire, the guards with machine
  guns ready to fire, the dry yellow

land and the tumbleweeds that roll around
  like herds of buffalo. The first

thing she'll see is not a pink wall, the smiling
    faces of nurses and doctors,

all she will see is the sad face of her mother
    and a photo of her father far away.

Like us. School started a week ago in Block 21,
    Hunt Junior High, on November 16.

My class is so big—there seem to be fifty or sixty of us,
    just calling out the roll takes forever.

Not that I'm complaining, but we don't have a blackboard or
    even enough books. We sit on picnic tables like we're

outside. We might as well be outside. If you're up front,
    you burn to death from the single pot-belly stove;

if you're in the back, you freeze to death. My teacher,
    Miss Clarendon, seems nice—just out of Stanford—

but she's sad that we don't all have textbooks and classes are cut
    short because there aren't enough classrooms.

Mom works in the mess hall.
    She earns $12 a month washing dishes, trays, forks

and knives. When she comes home late at night,
    barely in time for the curfew, she comes in tired,

with red, chapped hands, wearing the night around her
    hunched shoulders. Her body's bent in half as if she

were still standing by the sink in front of all of those
    dishes. She sighs a great sigh, and without taking off

her shoes, she sits on the cot, takes her shirt off, then
    her skirt, and asks for the hand cream she bought from

the Sears and Roebuck catalog last month with her first
    paycheck. Her very first. Some nights, she comes home,

tired, too tired even to use the cream for her hands, too
    tired even to wish me goodnight.

Tonight she lies down on the creaking cot
    with her clothes on, snoring as soon as her head hits the pillow.

Nick doesn't talk to us anymore. He's gone before
    I wake up; he comes in after the curfew.

The only person who seems himself is Grandpa.
    I miss you. I miss my family.

      Your Daughter, Mina Masako

NOVEMBER 1942

The air has been carrying the hint of angry
winter with it for the past two mornings.
When we woke up this morning, our breath turned

white like the solid columns of our house
back in Seattle, and when Mother opened
the window, the ground was completely covered

in snow, so white that it stung my eyes.
The yellow earth was covered; our barracks
were white, and even the barbed wire was white,

making me think, just for a second, that
I was looking at a white vine
with white berries strung unevenly along it.

Nick, Nick, look! I yelled, but Nick just turned
away from me, turning his back toward me
and the room—our home. I ran outside,

and looked up the sky, where the sun was white,
where flakes kept falling and falling, each snow
flake a perfect many-pointed star,

melting as soon as they landed on my hand.
Each step left a perfect footprint, leading from home
to somewhere, uneven, toward the irrigation.

The sun wasn't glaring; it was so much kinder, and so
soothing that I almost forgot Nick's darkness
and the darkness of the room that we'd made our home.

DECEMBER 1942

Our family is shredded like small dresses that Mother cuts
up to make brooms. Nick doesn't come home and no one knows
what he does all day. Mom works in the mess hall, washing

one dish after another, her hands getting redder and redder.
She doesn't smile anymore. But Grandpa's a snail with all
he needs on his back; he jokes with the other old

men in Japanese, though he says he misses working with
the land. Dad is far away, his letters criss-crossed by black
markers across his words. We are puzzle pieces, unwhole and apart.

DECEMBER 1942

Mina M. Tagawa
Miss Claredon 8th Core
December 29, 1942

"One Year Ago"

One year ago, Japanese attacked Pearl Harbor, and it
broke all our hearts. It is the day that changed my life,
though I'm sure it is the day that changed all Americans'
lives. I remember I was practicing with the church choir,
when the news of Pearl Harbor came.

After that, everything changed. Some Japanese American
men, like my father and our family friends, were taken
away by the immigration agency as "dangerous aliens."
Then came the curfew from 8pm to 6am, so we all stayed
inside, even our cat, Basho. Still, most of my friends in
Seattle were nice to me.

Then came the order to evacuate to Puyallup. We packed
everything quickly, and boarded the bus on April 29th—
our zone was one of the last ones to leave–while friends
saw us off. It made me very sad to leave my best friend,
Jamie Gilmore, and Basho. We stayed at Puyallup until
the end of August, when we were told to move to Idaho.
Our block was one of the first ones to leave. We got on the
train; the landscape looked very beautiful, but the closer
we got to Hunt, the worse it got. It was all sage bushes
and dry land and hot air. And now, here we are, in

barracks half finished, with no hot water, and dust everywhere. I thought Puyallup was bad, but this is much worse. School started in November. We also had our first snow, our first Thanksgiving and now, Christmas. This is our home away from home, and we have to make the best of it.

Christmas here seemed like every other ordinary day. Still, we celebrated in a very small way. All Americans are going through a little of what we are going through. I pray that the war will be over soon, and that we can all go home.

JANUARY 1943

Miss Claredon tells us
that we can't speak Japanese
at school anymore.
We all have to learn
to become more American, she says.
From this day on,
she'll give us American names.
So we can be more American,
she says. So we will be less
the enemy alien.

FEBRUARY 1943

When Father came back to us, he carried
the weight of the sky on his back.
When Father came home, he walked stooped,

his steps in the rhythm of a broken wheelbarrow,
his legs so skinny that his pant legs seem
only half filled, wanting for more.

He climbed down from the bus,
one step at a time, just like Grandpa,
though they are separated by four decades.

When Father's foot reached the ground,
Grandpa looked away as if he were looking into the sun,
as if the sight blinded and pained him;

then, in the same rhythm, Father and Grandpa
ran toward each other, then fell into each
other's arms, their circle so tight that Mother

and Nick and I could not enter, but just watch.
When Father came home, he slept through the day,
through the night, through the week,

and Mother stayed by his side under the dim
light, praying each hour, thanking Jesus
for his safe return. And when Father awoke,

he did not say anything about Montana. He did not
say anything about what had been left
out of his blackened letters; he did not say

anything. He sat by the window and drank
in the new landscape of our new home, he sat
with his eyes not understanding, almost

disappearing in the sunlight, so light he was.

FEBRUARY 1943

Dear Jamie,
Now that Father is home
Mother says that everything
is going to be okay.
Now that Father is home
Mother says that we can decide
what to do next.
Nick says that Father is
a coward; that's why he got
out of prison
earlier than any one else.
But I don't think so. He didn't
do anything wrong. What's wrong
is how he's aged:
his face, so lined
and his hair so shocked
with gray. The lines around
his face are as deep as the dry
ground in Minidoka.
Jamie, I still wear
the half heart. Do you?
My heart *is* broken.
I miss you very much.
There's no one like you
at school.
Your best friend, Mina

MARCH 1943

Masako, earth is a lot like people,
Grandpa says. Earth must be cared for,
tended. With patience, he says, you can
change a poor soil into a fertile
and rich soil, dark as chocolate and
so moist and rich that worms will
make it home, so tasty that when you chew
on it, the earth tastes sweet,
as sweet as sticky rice prepared to celebrate the new year.
This earth here, he says, has a chance
to become magnificent, and with time can become
rich and heavy. It just takes time,
it just takes patience, he says,
just like it does with people. Don't give up
until you have done everything to change
yourself. Then, he says as he sits
on the doorstep, only then can you start
blaming others.

MARCH 1943

I pledge
allegiance
to the flag
(we move
our mouths
as one)
of the United
States
of America,
(with our
hands over
our hearts)
and to the republic
for which it stands:
one nation, indivisible,
(we move
our mouths,
but our
words are
quiet)
with Liberty and
Justice
(we move
our mouths
as one)
for *all*.

APRIL 1943

Nick sits in a corner
bruised like a tomato,
not saying a word.
He broods; he sulks,
carrying the dark
cloud into the room
into his corner, casting
a dark shadow over all
of us. My father does
not say a word
as he writes in the notebook,
an article for the *Minidoka
Irrigator.* My mother pretends
nothing is wrong
as she massages Grandpa's
thin shoulders. I want
to scream, I want to say
anything, something,
yell at them, *Look at me,
look at Nick, do something!*
but I also pretend
that nothing is wrong
as I do my homework.
Nick's anger weighs
heavy like buzzing of mosquitoes.
The night is dark.
The coyotes howl so
close by, waiting for us
to come out, their howls

mixing in with the foul
smell from the irrigations
simmering, about
to explode.

APRIL 1943

No. 27. Are you willing to serve in the Armed forces of the
United States on combat duty wherever ordered?

Yes (I will fight, Nick says).

Yes (I will serve, Nick says, I'm so angry at you,
America, but I'll show you, I'll show you that I'm better than you.)

No (not until we are all Americans, Father says).

Yes (to prove that I am loyal, Shig, Nick's best friend says).

Yes (to prove that I am not an enemy, Nick says, so I can show you
I'm more American than those damn honkies who called me Jap).

No (I am not free, Father says).

Yes (yes, I am an American, Nick says).

No. 28. Will you swear unqualified allegiance to the
United States of America and faithfully defend the United
States from any or all attack by foreign or domestic forces,
and forswear any form of allegiance or obedience to the
Japanese emperor, to any other foreign government,
power or organization?

Yes (this is my home, Nick says).

Yes (America the free, *Oh say can you see…*, I pledge).

Yes (I pledge allegiance, to the flag, we say every morning.)

No (My father is Japanese, Father says, and this question is a trick question. There is only yes to one and no to the other, there is no and there is yes, and there is only no).

No (My grandfather was denied naturalization, Gary Kunieda says).

Yes (I'll defend you even if you don't want me to, I'll defend you America, because I'm an American, I'm not a Jap, Nick says).

Yes (I am an American, I say).

APRIL 1943

Everywhere there are shouts,
rattling of windows and doors.
Every night, and sometimes during the day,
shouts of people erupt like dust
storms, expected but surprising,
arguing about the questionnaire:
Are you willing to serve?
Nick and Father shout at meetings,
at each other. *Don't you dare
answer that question "yes," Nick,*
Father yells, *I didn't raise you to die in the war.
America doesn't trust us, so why should we help them?
How can you think of answering "yes"
after what our family's gone through?*
But Nick yells back, *I'm an American,
I will die for this country,
just to prove that we are loyal,
we are loyal even when they don't trust us.*
Their shouts make the floorboards
creak, and the walls tremble. Even dust
stays huddled in corners, in fear.
The night seems more alive than ever,
filled with angry words, and banging
doors and sobs. My brother will
die for a country that does not love us back.

APRIL 1943

Mr. and Mrs. Simon Kunieda's only
son has renounced his citizenship.
Every night for the past three weeks,
we heard them fighting
from three apartments down,
Mr. Simon Kunieda yelling
in a mixture of Japanese and English,
(more in Japanese as he gets excited),
with his son, Gary, yelling
only in English. Gary is to leave
the camp and then for Japan
in few days. I can hear Nick
breathing, sighing in the dark,
and Father's quiet voice,
breaking the night
into pieces with his low
whisper, *Nick, you are not to
do what Gary Kunieda did,
you hear me, son?*

MAY 1943

The way to school is dusty, a long
dusty stretch of road that goes from north
to south, an exacting compass that stretches

in a straight line, made by men
whose intentions were clear, sure.
The way to school is unforgiving.

When it rains, the road becomes knee-
deep with mud, and when it dries, forget
yesterday's rain. Forget about moisture.

Tumbleweeds own the streets, rolling
after us like dogs barking,
hurrying us to school. Getting to school

takes twenty minutes;
it's one straight line, both
sides adorned with never-ending barracks,

windows, eyes looking at us. The way to school
is always the same: yesterday, tomorrow,
today, next year, maybe forever.

JUNE 1943

Nick's diploma arrived in a brown envelope,
Special Delivery, with a note from Mrs. Campbell,

his senior homeroom teacher, "Nick, we missed you at
graduation. We miss your sense of humor and your laughter.

I am praying for this war to end as soon as possible. Some
of your friends missed graduation, too, since they've

volunteered already: Neal Higgins, Kevin Clark, Sammy
Walker."

Without looking, he took the diploma and ripped it
into shreds, then stomped on it. Mother screamed, "No, no!"

I saw his hurt so big and so raw. Without looking back,
he yelled, "This is what America is all about!" and went

through the door, entering the dust, disappearing amidst
the swirl of yellow, banging the door behind him,

followed by the ghostly sigh of Mr. Akagi.
Grandpa sighing from his corner, got his cane, and left

the room, quietly closing the door behind him.
Mother picked up the pieces strewn all over the room

like snow. I straightened the brown envelope,
and we glued each piece, one piece at a time

with leftover rice, onto the crinkled brown paper,
until Nick's name became whole, Nicholas Toshio Tagawa.

His diploma that could have taken him to the University
of Washington this September 1943.

AUGUST 1943

The first batch
of roses smothered
under the sandstorm
except for the one
Grandpa kept
beside his bed.
Even the red ones
that he had covered
with mosquito nets
were coated with gritty sand
so fine that they turned
white.
Grandpa sighs
and says that
there's next year,
and in the meanwhile,
he can help with
the field, all 420 acres
cultivated with hands
and bodies bent
with hopes so strong
they can and will change the soil.

SEPTEMBER 1943

Dear Jamie,
Nick and Father have been
fighting.
I was angry
for a very long time,
(I still am)
about what the government
did, about Father being
taken away, but when I think
about Gary Kunieda, I don't know
whether he did the right
thing either. He speaks
Japanese like a five-year-old;
I can't imagine why he wanted
to go to Japan. Father says that
it's unconstitutional to lock
people up without *due
process*; Nick thinks we need to
prove ourselves.
Our school year started,
and still there's no library,
no gym, just the same ol'
walk, the same ol' classroom
with no real desks.
We have a new teacher, though—
Miss Straub, not at all like
Miss Claredon. She sort of
reminds me of a bird,
that albatross like the one we used to see

on the wharf, remember?
So big but so beautiful in the sky.
She says that she's going
to call us by what we want
to be called. She didn't pronounce
"Masako" like teachers back home,
but pronounced it like Grandpa,
each sound weighing the same.
She said that it was a beautiful
name; she said that Mina was beautiful.
She says that
we have to study hard
because this isn't going to
last long, that we have
to think of tomorrow.
She also brought us lots of books,
she practically started
a library for us.
I get the feeling
that this year is going to be
different, maybe better
than last year.

                Your best friend, Mina Masako

OCTOBER 1943

Grandpa kneels
in his garden,
readying the roses
for winter.
He sings quietly,
a tune without words,
words lost somewhere
between Japan
and here,
left behind
in Seattle.

NOVEMBER 1943

Mina Masako Tagawa
November 16, 1943
Miss Straub's 9th Core
Civics

"What It Means to Be an American"

What it means to be an American is the question I
have been asking myself for the past year and half. I am
sure that other Americans of Japanese ancestry who have
been moved from the West Coast to ten concentration
camps in the United States have been asking the same
question, too.

My father was arrested right after the Japanese attack on
Pearl Harbor. He was put in prison, and lost a lot of weight
during his imprisonment. Even today, we are not sure
why he was arrested. But he was also not the only person
who was arrested. There were many men like him all over
America, Americans just like my father, who were arrested
and imprisoned without the proper procedure of law.

When we were first moved to Camp Harmony in April
1942, we were told to pack only what we could carry. We
were given name tags to wear as if we were no longer
human, but were luggage, or animals. The government
took away our names, our houses, and most importantly,
our dignity. We had to live in former stalls where horses
used to be; we lived in less than acceptable living
conditions. When they moved us again in August 1942

to Minidoka, where we are now, we did not know what would happen to us. There were all kinds of rumors: that we would be shot; that food they served us on the trains would be poisoned.

It was very hard when we first got here, but things are better now. Everyone helped in building real bathrooms, a swimming pond, irrigations, and now, a beautiful farm full of vegetables and fruits. It is not the same as Seattle, where it rains and where it's warm and so green. But we are trying to get as close to what we left behind as we can. I am not sure what it means to be an American but I am learning.

NOVEMBER 1943

Nick comes home
his eyes shining like
Basho's when he comes
home with a tuft
of feather
in his mouth.
Nick, without saying
a word, sits down
next to Father. And he
looks at his hands
for a long time,
like he is thinking,
like he wants to
say something
but words are hiding
somewhere inside
of his throat. Then
he coughs. *Dad*, Nick
says, *there's an Army*
unit for boys like me,
the U.S. Army created
a unit just for Japanese
boys so that we can fight
the Nazis and fascists
and maybe the Japanese.
Dad, I'm going
to volunteer as soon
as I turn eighteen
in January.

Father stops
polishing his shoes.
Mother stops
mending a pant leg.
Father looks slowly
at Nick.
Nick looks down
at his hand again.
Nick, if you ever volunteer,
Father says without
moving his lips,
*after all that we've gone
through, if you ever
volunteer, you'll have to do
it over my dead body.*
And Father continues to work
like he never spoke,
the only sound in the room
the fast
staccato sound of the brush
bristling against worn leather.

DECEMBER 1943

The room shook.
Father changed in front
of my eyes and punched
Nick, and Mother screamed.
Nick overturned the table,
breaking the leg,
and Grandpa jumped up
from his bed, thrusting
his cane between Father
and Nick. Nick raised
his arm and Father tried
to punch Nick again,
and the three of them were
suddenly dancing fast and furiously
to the sound
of a drummer's beat. From
one wall to another, Grandpa's
glasses flew through the air,
and landed by my feet, cracking,
and Nick yelled, *You are a coward, you're*
a spineless coward; you think
that if you're like a good Japanese,
pretending nothing is wrong,
saying shikataganai—*shrugging*
your shoulder, can't be helped,
everything will be all right.
It's men like you, who don't fight back,
that made this mess.
Well, I'm sick

of it, I'm sick of all this,
I'm going to prove to you,
and to everyone, that I'm
a man, that I'm an American
just like those honkies
that call me a Jap boy.
Father dropped his arm
to his side. Grandpa held
Nick, taking him outside.
Mother cried and I stood
in the corner, shaking.
Grandpa's glasses lay
on the floor, cracked.

Part IV. Minidoka Relocation Center
Hunt, Idaho
JANUARY 1944

The bus waits
outside the gate.
Nick stands straight,
his face suddenly
like Father's, older,
taller, bigger than
I remember him.
Father is still angry;
he is in bed.
Nick smiles wide,
His *Seattle* smile.
Grandpa holds out
his hand, *Nihondanji*
No na o kegasuna
(don't shame the reputation
of Japanese men),
rippa ni tatakatte koi
(fight well and make
us proud).
Nick laughs so loud that
he almost blew
away the guards above the tower.
He almost shatters the sky
with his ready laugh.
The bus honks.
Nick hugs us quickly,
then walks away
with his back straight,

so tall and almost
a soldier already.
Zettai Ikite kaette koi
(you must come back
alive) Grandpa shouts.
Zettai ikite kaette koi,
I whisper.

FEBRUARY 1944

Dear Mina,

I got your letter yesterday, and it's good to hear that everyone's doing well back in the camp. We arrived in Mississippi, the boys and I. Shig nearly died trying to get off the bus with a bag that was bigger than him, but we arrived all in one piece. The train to the south was long and you wouldn't believe how humid it is here, so unlike Idaho. But you know, I don't miss it. If anything, I miss Seattle, the sea, the food, and all that. They gave us another physical, we stood in this line and then that line (it's good to be home). Then it's been non-stop on the go—being woken up before the sun, running, eating, running, shooting. Food's not bad, not like in our block's back home. But it's the lack of sleep that's getting to me. Shig and I went into the town near Camp Shelby, and Shig had to go to the bathroom real bad, but we just couldn't figure out which bathroom to use: the one for white, or the one for negroes. So I went up to the gas station owner, and asked as politely as I could, "Which one should we use?" The old man there was really confused, too, kept looking at me, trying to figure out the same question. Then he said, "suppose the white one." Shig and I had a good laugh about it—here, down South, we're not Japanese like we were back in Seattle, but white. Before I forget, thank Mom for the sweater, I know how hard it is to find yarn. Tell her I'm doing well, and that there's nothing to worry about. Tell Dad that it seems like we may be shipped to Europe, instead of the Pacific, like he thought we would be—or that's what other boys tell me. Hope he's not angry with me anymore. Tell him that I'll make him proud. Tell Grandpa not to work too much; that old boy can be in the garden like a fifteen year old, but the sun is hot and he's getting old. Tell them that all the boys and I are here to fight, and we're ready to fight for our country. I'm sending you some bars of soap and chocolates—send my love, and I'll write you more when I have more time.

Your loving brother, Nick

MARCH 1944

Father does not
speak as he goes
about his days,
working at the newspaper.
Mom's hands,
as red and chapped as rotten
plums, move busily
knitting a scarf for Nick.
Grandpa coughs a hollow
cough, once, twice,
again and again,
until his entire body trembles.

APRIL 1944

Miss Straub almost sings.
Hope is the thing with feathers
that perches in the soul,
and sings the tune without the words,
and never stops at all.
And the words keep flying out of Miss Straub's mouth,
and Emily Dickinson keeps singing
and I close my eyes
and Miss Straub closes her book.

MAY 1944

The sun glares down on top of us,
my father, my mother, and Grandpa.
We are in a row of four,
from east to west,
as we till the ground.

The water from irrigation feeds the land.
    We tame the land with our hands, with Grandpa's
    dream to make this land as green as Seattle, greener
    and darker, banishing the tumbleweeds.

The sun is strong,
our shadows darker
the darkest of dark.
There is no sound.
The earth is dry,

    the sky so stark blue with white
    clouds the size of two barracks put together.
    We measure Grandpa's dream with earth,
    changing the land from dusk-yellow to darkest brown.

Grandpa sings,
he is the farmer, the gardener,
the guardian of this land.
Grandpa sings,
We must be patient,

with our dreams. The land will listen. The land will dream. The land will sing itself to sleep, and when it wakes up, it will be fertile, and roots will take roots.
We will make this our land, our home.

JUNE 1944

The first soldier from the camp
    came back yesterday
as an American flag, folded.
    Yesterday, Tadaharu "Ted"
Komiya, quarterback for the University
    of Washington, came home,
dead. The only son of Mr. and Mrs. Komiya
    in Area B. He came back
without a body. Only a purple star
    and a letter of regret.
The whole mess hall had a moment of silence
    to grieve for him.

JULY 1944

Dear Nick,

After you left
    for Mississippi, the roses
finally blossomed in colors of pink, red,
     white…and even light blue.
Remember when Grandpa told us his
    dream about growing blue roses?
People from miles away
    come to buy Grandpa's roses,
even the guards on their days off.
    Father is getting better.
More and more, he's helping Grandpa
    with the rose garden like he used to
back home. Mother is well;
    she's still working in the kitchen.
Grandpa can't stop coughing,
    I worry about him.
We're trying to stay
    cheerful, though it's not
the same without you.
    Miss Straub, my new
teacher, has been talking to us
    about what it means to be
an American. She says that it doesn't
    matter who we are—a man, a woman
negro, oriental, old, young.
    None of that matters.

What matters is whether we are being
    the best person we know how to be
at any given time. Don't get yourself
    killed. We are waiting for the war to end
so you can come back to us.
    I miss you. And I'm so proud of you.

      Your sister, Mina Masako

JULY 1944

Dear Jamie,
I'm sure I told you
Nick's volunteered.
He's written a couple
of times, saying he's doing
well. You know Nick.
He's so cheerful most
of the time (well, at least
back in Seattle) and I think
he is much happier now
than he was in the camp.
Father was pretty upset
but like a "good Japanese,"
he eventually shrugged
and said, *shikataganai*—can't be helped.
It's so strange to be
here, even after two years.
I feel more American now
than I ever did.
But there's also a very strong
Japanese-ness here, too. Like
living quietly so we don't
bother others, like helping
each other out when we can.
We've been talking a lot
about what it means
to be an American. I wrote
an awful essay for Miss Straub,
then we debated about it for months.

And slowly, I'm beginning to understand.
America tells us
you're not American
but the country also asks us
to fight and maybe *die*
to protect it.
We say the Pledge,
we buy the war
bonds, we help
with the war effort,
and men like my brother
have enlisted
and are fighting.
But we do it
because we love our home.
Because home isn't just
our family, but it's something bigger,
it's everything and everyone,
and even when we fight,
even when we hurt each other,
we are family, no matter what.
Maybe that's what America is for me.
I almost feel like this is home.

     Your best friend, Mina Masako

SEPTEMBER 1944

When an old person
goes into the hospital,
they go in to die. I see it
whenever I go to
the hospital with Grandpa
for his check-ups.
The hospital is full of
old people, with their eyes
dull like three-day dead
fish on the market stall,
the kind of fish
no one would eat
except for flies.
The hospital is full of
old people, with their bodies
giving up on walking and talking.
Grandpa's eyes
are still bright.
He has not given up yet.

OCTOBER 1944

Barracks that used
to be full
like beehives
are now empty.
Families, one
after another,
are leaving
with crisp letters
of permission
to relocate to
Chicago or
to the East Coast.
Mother looks out
the window,
counting how many
families are left.
Father looks down
at the article
he is writing.
The rose garden
in front of our room
is resting.
This is our home.

NOVEMBER 1944

5 Men killed, 15 Wounded
in Southern France
the first page of the *Minidoka*
Irrigator screams.
I scan for Nick,
for anyone we know.
We only see Shig
"slightly wounded,"
but it's a different Shig.
No mention of Nick.
Mother sighs with relief,
and Grandpa doesn't say
anything. Please, God,
make him come back alive,
I don't care if he gets
medals, I don't care
if he makes us proud,
just let him come back
to us alive.

DECEMBER 1944

I do not want to see Grandpa lying
on the hospital bed, his arms thin and spotted
as if he has all the sun in the world on his skin.
I do not want to see Grandpa lying
on the hospital bed, his eyes closed
like he is dreaming,
like he doesn't care about us anymore.
I stand by the doorway of the dark room,
I tiptoe over, not to wake him.
The western corner of his lip curls
into a smile and he says, without opening
his eyes, *Toshio wa buji darou ka?*
—I wonder if Toshio is all right?
I go over. He is so pale, he almost seems
to melt into the sunlight if not for
his bones still beneath the skin,
if not for the suns swirling on his arms.

JANUARY 1945

Masako,
Grandpa speaks,
his voice like a candle
about to flicker
out, Masako, don't
forget that you are
an American, and you're
Japanese. You have
two halves in one
soul, one that is
America, like this land,
and one that is
Japan. You are Masako,
but you're also Mina.
I can't offer
you an answer,
but your job is
to learn to live
with these two
broken pieces
and to make them one.
He raises his arm
slowly, then fingers my necklace,
the half-broken heart.
Just like this heart,
he whispers,
just like this.

FEBRUARY 1945

My grandfather lies shrouded on his bed,
    but his soul does not live in his body

anymore. Incense burns. Mother has been keeping vigil,
    reciting the psalms, then the only Buddhist sutra

she knows. "He is Japanese, his last journey
    should be in Japanese, too. How will he find

his way to heaven without Japanese?" she says.
    Father sits on the porch step outside

quiet, quieter than the time Nick left, quieter than the
    time he came back from Montana. He smokes

one cigarette after another, exhaling smoke from his
    half-opened mouth as if he is sending off

Grandpa's soul toward the sky. Mother said that Father found
    Grandpa kneeling by the roses in his hospital

pajamas as if he were tasting
    the soil like he used to, his hands on

the earth, feeling the heat that's been absorbed
    from the sun. Mother said that when Father tapped him

on his shoulder, Grandpa just kneeled deeper as if he was
    praying. As if he were listening to the ground

move beneath him. But he was dead already.
    Mother said that when they brought Grandpa back,

the rose was held tightly in his hand.
    He died in his garden, where he felt at home.

He died with his hands and feet caked in mud, with a rose
    in his hand. He died amidst the roses, away

from the dark and dank hospital room, away from our sad
    room, away from the land of his birth,

away from Seattle, away from us,
    quietly surrounded by the only thing he brought from
    home: roses.

FEBRUARY 1944

Dear Jamie,

Thank you for your letter.
Grandpa would have loved the news
about the cherry blossom tree.
Tell your father that Grandpa always
appreciated him for taking care of the house.
I never thought that he would die.
I never knew how much it would hurt.
I would be doing my homework,
and suddenly, I think Grandpa is lying
on his bed like he used to,
and I would start to tell him about my day
until I remember that he is gone.
And all this sadness, all this grief
comes rushing out, and I cry.
And there will be no one around
so I go to Grandpa's bed,
and lie down and I can smell him still:
the smell of earth and dirt and a little
bit of rose. And I cry and cry
until I can't breath anymore
and I think I'm going to die
and I don't care if I do.
Jamie, I never knew I could hurt so much.
                    Mina Masako

MARCH 1945

Dear Mina,

This is a letter I can't send to you, but I am writing to let
you know that I am alive. Even now, I'm surprised that I
lived after two weeks of hell through mud and rain and
bullets. They told us that the Germans had fortified the
hill, and that our battalion was supposed to take it. We'd
been crawling on our stomachs through the mud, marching
through the rain, fighting, fighting for the past week and
half, and now, they want us to fight, again. Lieutenant
Kawahata didn't say anything when he got the message, but
just said, "Boys, we've got another job." One by one, the
boys shot through the barren landscape between us and the
hill, and one by one, they got shot down. Like toy soldiers
being flicked off a board. Like I used to, when I was a kid.
Shig fell screaming. Kaz fell. Bob fell, they all fell, littering
the ground, some so quiet, some screaming for help. One
by one, my friends fell, and the only thing I could do was
to keep the artillery shells going, aiming at the hill where
snipers might be, until finally, Kot got through—he's always
been the fastest and the smallest, and shot down the closest
sniper. The path became clear and opened up. The zigzag
through the earth seemed impossible. I was shaking, I was
scared. So goddamn scared. Then Lieutenant Kawahata
shot through the zigzag, then one boy after another, following
the impossible zigzag toward the hill, following Kot's path
while I kept pumping shell after shell on the impossible hill.
And it became easy. We all made it through, though we lost
half the boys that day. It was our first real victory, but I felt
as if we had lost this whole stinking war. With Kaz gone.

Really gone. Shig may have to live with one leg for the rest of his life. When the Germans surrendered with their arms raised high, holding a white flag, they weren't at all how I imagined them: hard, cruel, tall and monstrous with cigars clamped between their jaws talking about how they wanted to shoot babies and old people. Instead they were boys like us, teenagers, tired, scared, dirty, and looking almost relieved that their war was over, for now, that they could rest their bone-tired bodies in the POW camp. But this war, for me, will keep going until the war ends, or until I die, whichever comes first. And I don't want to die like Kaz, left in the middle of the field screaming until we couldn't hear him. By the time we got there, it was too late. He died all alone. I don't want to die like that. I don't want to die at all. It's a beautiful night tonight. Boys and I are in a small village in Italy, right near the French border, drinking wine and smoking. No one is saying much. But I think we are all thinking the same thing: we don't want to die; we want this war to be over. Most of the time, we are walking or fighting or cold or hungry, but in times like this, when it's all quiet, I tell myself that I'm fighting for you, so that you don't have to walk down the street ashamed of who you are, so that you can be free, but I don't know what that means. I so goddamn wish that this was a dream. When we wake up, we're all back in our house, not the camp, but our house, in Seattle, with Mom and Dad and Grandpa and you.

Your brother, Nick.

APRIL 1945

The sky without Grandpa
    is empty.
The room without Grandpa
    is unfamiliar.
Life without Grandpa
    has no laughter.
Roses are dull. Birds no
    longer sing.
Our family is torn apart:
    Nick is away,
fighting the war,
    Father is quiet
in his sadness,
    Mother doesn't talk
as much as she used to,
    and I feel
more alone than I have
    ever felt.

APRIL 1945

Dear Mina,

    This is not a letter you will ever read.
This is a letter I will never send you.
Today, we opened the gates of hell.
As we approached the camp,
scarecrows, or so we thought, began to cheer,
and we knew then, that these weren't scarecrows
or skeletons, but men so skinny their clothes
barely hung on their bones. More of them came out,
limping, ghost-like, wearing identical
striped shirts and pants. None of us could
speak. We've never seen anything like this—
this nightmare—in our lives,
not in a battlefield,
not in the villages we marched through.
One old man sat slumped against a barrack,
his eyes barely open. I thought he was old
until I saw his face; he was my age,
though most of his teeth had rotted,
and his body was so skinny he weighed less
than you do. It was snowing
but he did not seem to care.
I forgot how cold it was. When I reached
over, he opened his eyes, so slowly, and smiled.
Then he sighed, and fell into my arms.
Just like that. And died.
This is hell, Mina, where men die as soon
as they are freed. This is hell when men do
this to each other. I never thought anything like

this was possible. I can't close my eyes; instead
of this place, I see the camp back
home, where you are, surrounded by barbed wire,
by guard towers, just like here, and you and Mom
and Dad as skinny, and horrible-looking,
as these men. They call this place
Dachau. This is hell. I don't know what war is
anymore. I don't understand anything. Is there
anything left to live for?
        Your brother, Nick.

VE DAY, 1945

A photo of sailors in the newspaper,
    smiling widely.
A man swoops a woman down to the ground, kissing
    her like they are in the middle
of a dance.

A photo of New York filled with so many flags
    and people that all the buildings
are hidden under the cheers I can't hear.
    Waves of flags, American flags
all in midair. Still.

A picture of a fat Italian man—Mussolini—
    hanging upside down
from a lamppost somewhere in Italy.
    Next to him are two more bodies, one a woman
and another a man.

A picture of German soldiers with
    their arms raised high, their eyes
downcast. A little girl with a white flag
    and an American flag, smiling.
The war has ended. Nick can come home.

JULY 1945

A woman killed her baby
today because she was
afraid of leaving the camp.
Her husband wrapped
the baby, her head
as soft as a rotten tomato,
and begged the doctors
to fix her. The baby
was dead. The mother
was afraid of leaving.

AUGUST 1945

The day the bomb fell on the city
    of Hiroshima, the sky here was so blue
that it hurt the eyes. The roses
    like beggars, waiting for water,
as men and women crouched on the ground,
    blinded by the sudden flash.
The day the bomb fell on Hiroshima, I was sitting
    on the porch with Father, looking at the gravestone
that sits lonely in the middle of the roses,
    wondering if Grandpa made it safely
to the otherworld, like they said all Japanese spirits
    do when they die. They take 49 days to travel
through the otherworld, and then they come back here.
    Where we are. Just to say that they are alright,
that they have seen the otherworld, and that it is going
    to be their new home. Just to say, they care.
And it has been more than 49 days, and Grandpa must be here
    amidst the roses, maybe even sitting
next to me. On the day the bomb fell, a lark scooped
    down from the sky, landed on a rose,
sang a keening note, just one, then flew away,
    breaking the sky into pieces.

SEPTEMBER 1945

We packed everything
we have into the trunks
and bags and crates
and closed the door
behind us. Father says
that we do not need to lock
the door. There is no
one to see us off.
The camp is deserted,
it's a ghost town,
a place lonely after the carnival.
There won't be school in the fall.
People have left already,
packing their worries
and their hopes that everything will
be the same when they go
home. Not go *back* home,
but to go home. After
three years, no one
goes *back*, they *go*.
Dad dug up Grandpa's roses
and transplanted them
into pots, some cracked,
some small, some big,
and the rest have to
survive on their own—
though spring will never
come and no one will
dig them out.

We have dug up Grandpa's
bones; like his roses,
we have packed Grandpa.
We are leaving our three
years behind. We are leaving
Minidoka, back to Seattle.

SEPTEMBER 1945

The streets throughout Seattle are the same
with people busily going about
their business as if nothing had ever changed.
My mother sings to herself.
The neighborhood is still the same,
with trees lining the block both left and right,
trees so bright red and yellow they hurt
my eyes. Our driveway is the same,
just as we left it, and my cherry blossom
tree stands with its bark gnarled.
Father honks the horn; Mr. Gilmore
waves from his window, and comes
out smiling, *Welcome home, welcome
home*. The third step to the front
door still creaks tiredly. The windows
are boarded up. Mr. Gilmore hugs Father
tight; Father hardens, then relaxes,
and puts his arms around Mr. Gilmore's
small round body. Jamie comes out
from the house, she runs down
with her arms open,
she rushes toward me, taller, blonder,
crying, *Mina, I missed you so much!*
And I start running, forgetting the hurt,
the ache I carried. I open my arms
and we hug each other, tight, never
to let go, finally our broken halves
becoming one, inseparable.

Epilogue
DECEMBER 1945

Dear Mina,

I am now stationed
in Tokyo to help with
the Occupation. That
came as a surprise,
but they needed Americans
who can speak
Japanese, to translate.
I had nothing else to do
in Europe, anyway.
Some boys told us that
when they went home
during their leave,
some honkies harassed
them. Even Lieutenant
Kawahara, with his purple
heart and all, was told
to get his Jap
ass out of the bus.
I figured America isn't
ready for me yet, so maybe
I'll try Japan.
Tokyo is exactly
like Dresden or Nuremberg:
completely bombed, destroyed.
You can see Tokyo from
one end to another,
it's so flattened out, so

black and burned.
Kids a little younger than
you run after us, yelling
chocolate, candy, please,
while people wearing rags
walk around, tired, exhausted,
but they seem almost happy, too.
It's pretty bad:
you see kids, three and four years old,
sitting on the street alone.
Some of them are dead,
but people just ignore them.
No one can help; everyone's hungry.
So I take these kids to orphanages.
I give them as much money as I can to
help them get through.
For the first time in a long
while, I feel like I am doing
something good, something besides
killing and…well, killing.
These kids call me *Oni-chan,*
big brother, and I think of you.
It's strange to be here;
everywhere, I see people
who look like me,
who look like Dad and Mom,
but to them, I am American.
Maybe it's the way I walk,
maybe it's my bad Japanese,

121

maybe it's my uniform,
but I don't look Japanese to them,
and I don't *feel*
Japanese. I know, more
than ever, I'm just an American,
pure and simple.

Your brother, Nick

ABOUT THE JAPANESE AMERICAN INTERNMENT

When I was growing up in San Francisco in the 1980s, our doctor was a second-generation Japanese American named Dr. William Kiyasu. He was a gentleman: he wore a bow tie and he was always kind and compassionate. My mother told me later that his family was in an internment camp during World War II. His story stayed with me, and when I was writing *Dust of Eden*, I kept thinking of Dr. Kiyasu and how he had endured a dark period in American history.

During World War II, more than 110,000 Japanese Americans were forced from their homes. President Franklin D. Roosevelt issued Executive Order 9066 in February 1942, three months after Japan's attack on Pearl Harbor in Hawaii and in response to prejudiced fears that Japanese Americans were spies. The entire West Coast population of Japanese Americans was evacuated. Two-thirds of them were American citizens. They were often given less than a month to sell their properties and put their affairs in order. Uprooted from their lives and tagged like luggage, they brought only what they could carry to the camps.

At the relocation camps, internees lived in cramped wooden barracks that lacked plumbing and adequate protection from heat and cold. What many remember most about the camp experience is standing in line—for mess hall, laundry, coupons, jobs. Yet internees strove to maintain a sense of normalcy by joining clubs, cultivating the desert land, and having parties.

The first-generation Japanese Americans, the Issei, tended to live by the stoic Japanese principle known as *gaman*, which means to bear hardship silently. The Nisei, the second-generation Japanese Americans, questioned the unfair treatment by the government. Nonetheless, many chose to remain loyal to America. Some internees volunteered to join the army, and despite the prejudices they faced, the Japanese American regiment became the most decorated infantry regiment in the history of the United States military.

When the war ended and internees left the camps in 1945, many found their homes occupied, their jobs gone, and were subjected to unfair treatment. It was not until 1988 that the U.S. government paid reparations to the surviving internees.